Jamaica Tag-Along

Jamaica Tag-Along

Juanita Havill

Illustrations by Anne Sibley O'Brien

Houghton Mifflin Company
Boston

For Matilda Welter
        —J.H.
For Perry and Yunhee
        —A.S.O'B.

Library of Congress Cataloging-in-Publication Data

Havill, Juanita.
    Jamaica tag-along.
    Summary: When her older brother refuses to let her tag along with him, Jamaica goes
off by herself and allows a younger child to play with her.
    ISBN 0-395-49602-0
    [1. Brothers and sisters—Fiction. 2. Friendship—Fiction. 3. Play—Fiction]
I. O'Brien, Anne Sibley, ill.   II. Title.
PZ7.H31115JaK   1989   88-13478
[E]

Text copyright © 1989 by Juanita Havill
Illustrations copyright © 1989 by Anne Sibley O'Brien

Printed in the United States of America

RNF ISBN 0-395-49602-0
PAP ISBN 0-395-54949-3

WOZ 30 29 28 27 26 25 24 23 22

Jamaica ran to the kitchen to answer the phone. But her brother got there first.

"It's for me," Ossie said.

Jamaica stayed and listened to him talk.

"Sure," Ossie said. "I'll meet you at the court."

Ossie got his basketball from the closet. "I'm going to shoot baskets with Buzz."

"Can I come, too?" Jamaica said. "I don't have anything to do."

"Ah, Jamaica, call up your own friends."

"Everybody is busy today."

"I don't want you tagging along."

"I don't want to tag along," Jamaica said. "I just want to play basketball with you and Buzz."

"You're not old enough. We want to play serious ball."

Ossie dribbled his basketball down the sidewalk. Jamaica followed at a distance on her bike.

Buzz was already at the school court, shooting baskets with Jed and Maurice.

She parked her bike by the bushes and crept to the corner of the school building to watch.

That's not fair, Jamaica thought. Maurice is shorter than I am.

Pom, pa-pom, pa-pom, pom, pom.

The boys started playing, Ossie and Jed against Buzz and Maurice.

Jamaica sneaked to the edge of the court.

Maurice missed a shot and the ball came bouncing toward her. Jamaica jumped. "I've got the ball," she yelled.

"Jamaica!" Ossie was so surprised he tripped over Buzz. They both fell down.

Jamaica dribbled to the basket and tossed the ball. It whirled around the rim and flew out.

"I almost made it," Jamaica shouted. "Can I be on your team, Ossie?"

"No. N-O, Jamaica. I told you not to tag along."

"It's not fair. You let Maurice play."

"We need two on a team. Why don't you go play on the swings and stay out of the way?"

"I still think it's not fair." Jamaica walked slowly over to the sandlot.

She started to swing, but a little boy kept walking in front of her. His mom should keep him out of the way, Jamaica thought.

She looked up and saw a woman pushing a baby back and forth in a stroller.

Jamaica sat down in the sand and began to dig. She made a big pile with the wet sand from underneath. She scooped sand from the mound to form a wall.

"Berto help," said the little boy. He sprinkled dry sand on the walls.
"Don't," said Jamaica. "You'll just mess it up." Jamaica turned her back.

She piled the wet sand high. She made a castle with towers. She dug a ditch around the wall.

Jamaica turned to see if Berto was still there. He stood watching. Then he tried to step over the ditch, and his foot smashed the wall.

"Stay away from my castle," Jamaica said.

"Berto," the woman pushing the stroller said, "leave this girl alone. Big kids don't like to be bothered by little kids."

"That's what my brother always says," Jamaica said. She started to repair the castle. Then she thought, but I don't like my brother to say that. It hurts my feelings.

Jamaica smoothed the wall. "See, Berto, like that. You can help me make a bigger castle if you're very careful."

Jamaica and Berto made a giant castle. They put water from the drinking fountain in the moat.

"Wow," Ossie said when the game was over and the other boys went home. "Need some help?"

"If you want to," Jamaica said.

Jamaica, Berto, and Ossie worked together on the castle.

Jamaica didn't even mind if Ossie tagged along.